To those twin rascals Julia and Biddy . . . I have often tried
to find you down the back of the chair—M.M.

For Lucy Neale, with love—P.D.

Clarion Books
a Houghton Mifflin Company imprint
215 Park Avenue South, New York, NY 10003

Text copyright © 2006 by Margaret Mahy
Illustrations copyright © 2006 by Polly Dunbar
First published in the United Kingdom in 2006 by Frances Lincoln Limited.
First American edition, 2006.

The illustrations were executed in watercolors and cut paper.
The text was set in 27-point Aunt Mildred.

For information about permission to reproduce selections from this book, write to Permissions,
Houghton Mifflin Company, 215 Park Avenue South, New York, NY 10003.

www.houghtonmifflinbooks.com

Printed in China

Library of Congress Cataloging-in-Publication Data
Mahy, Margaret.
Down the back of the chair / Margaret Mahy ; illustrated by Polly Dunbar.—1st American ed.
    p. cm.
Summary: A poor family is searching down the back of a chair for Dad's lost car keys and,
miraculously in the mess of things back there, their financial problems are solved.
ISBN 0-618-69395-5
[1. Chairs—Fiction. 2. Lost and found possessions—Fiction.
3. Poor—Fiction. 4. Stories in rhyme.]   I. Dunbar, Polly, ill. II. Title.
PZ8.3.M278Dow 2006
[E]—dc22   2005017616

ISBN-13: 978-0-618-69395-5
ISBN-10: 0-618-69395-5

10 9 8 7 6 5 4 3 2 1

DOWN THE BACK OF THE CHAIR

Margaret Mahy

Illustrated by

Polly Dunbar

Clarion Books

New York

Our car is slow to start and go.
We can't afford a new one.
Now, if you please, Dad's lost the keys.
We're facing rack and ruin.

No car, no work! No work, no pay!

We're growing poorer day by day.

No wonder Dad is turning gray.

This morning is a blue one.

Nothing but dockets
in his pockets,
raging with despair,

Dad acts appalled!
Though nearly bald,
he tries to tear his hair.

8

But Mary,
who is barely two,
says, "Dad should do
what I would do!

I lose a lot, but I find a few—
down the back of the chair."

He's patted himself and searched the shelf.
He's hunted here and there,
so now he'll kneel and try to feel
right down the back of the chair.

Oh, it seemed to grin as his hand went in.
He felt tingling under his skin.
What will a troubled father win
from down the back of the chair?

Some hairy string and a diamond ring

were down the back of the chair.

Pineapple peel and a conger eel

were down the back of the chair.

A sip, a sup, a sop, a song, a spider seven inches long.

No wonder that it smells so strong— down the back of the chair.

A packet of pins
and **one of the twins,**
down the back of the chair.

A pan, a fan that belonged to Gran,

down the back of the chair....

A crumb,

a comb,

a clown,

a cap,

a pirate with a **treasure** map,

a dragon trying to take a nap—

down the back

of the chair.

A cake, a drake, a smiling snake,

down the back of the chair.

A string of pearls,
a lion with curls,
down the back
of the chair.

A skink, a skunk, a skate, a ski,

a couple of elephants

drinking tea,

a bandicoot and a bumblebee, down the back of the chair.

But what is this?

Oh, bliss! Oh, bliss!

Down the back of the chair.

The long lost will

of Uncle Bill,

down the back

of the chair.

His **money box** all crammed with **cash**,
tangled up in a **scarlet sash**.
There's **pleasure**, **treasure**, **toys**, and **trash**—
down the back of the chair.

"I've found my dreams,"

our father beams,

"down the back of the chair.

At last I see

how life can be,

down the back

of the chair."

"Forget the keys! We're poor no more.
Just call a taxi to the door."

A taxi shot out with a roar

from down the back of the chair.

The chair
the chair,

the challenging chair,

the champion chair, the cheerful chair,

the charming chair, the children's chair,

the chopped and chipped but chosen chair.

To think our fortune
waited there—

down the back
of the
chair!